FOOTBALL STORIES

Also by Michael Coleman

FIZZY HITS THE HEADLINES
FIZZY STEALS THE SHOW
FIZZY T.V. STAR

ORCHARD BOOKS
96 Leonard Street, London EC2A 4RH
Orchard Books Australia
14 Mars Road, Lane Cove, NSW 2066
ISBN 1 85213 739 8 (hardback)
ISBN 1 85213 949 8 (paperback)
First published in Great Britain 1994 as *Redville Rockets*
First paperback publication 1997
Text © Michael Coleman 1994
Illustrations © Ant Parker 1994
The right of Michael Coleman to be identified as the author
and Ant Parker as the illustrator of this work has been
asserted by them in accordance with the Copyright,
Designs and Patents Act, 1988.
A CIP catalogue record for this book is available from the
British Library.
Printed in Great Britain

FOOTBALL STORIES

Michael Coleman
Illustrated by Ant Parker

ORCHARD BOOKS

CONTENTS

Round 5
Redville Rockets v. Pridwell Pride
Right Back - Behind the Goal

Semi-Final
Redville Rockets v. Lansdowne Lions
It's Tough Having Your 'Tonsils' Out

The Final
Redville Rockets v. Jarrett Juniors

Come on, Number 12!

REDVILLE

1 Roly Bentall

3 Jenny Thorpe

2 Ian "Mad Max" Maxwell

4 Ramona "Sis" Gupta

6 Matt Pickup

5 Ramon "Bruv" Gupta

ROCKETS

8 Katie Sparks

7 Steve "Tonsils" Thomas (Capt)

9 Winston "Cannonball" Carter

0 Ben Wilkins

11 Jason Legge

12 Edwin Leek

Manager: Mr Sidney "Knees-Up" Knebworth

Mr. S. Knebworth
Redville School
Redville Lane
Redville

Dear Mr. Knebworth

INTER-SCHOOLS CUP

Thank you for your completed entry form and entry fee. I hereby confirm that:

REDVILLE ROCKETS

have been duly entered in this year's Inter-Schools Cup competition.

Good Luck!

Yours in football

Ivor Boot.

Secretary

REDVILLE ROCKETS V. RIPLEY RANGERS

Roly Gets it Together

"Come out, Roly! Come out!"

Roly Bentall didn't need telling. As the forward raced through, the ball at his toes, Roly was already scurrying out of his goal.

All the tips from his favourite book, *Be a Better Goalkeeper*, crowded into his mind. "Stay on your feet. Narrow the angle. Keep your eye on the ball..."

No problem, thought Roly as the forward took his shot. His angle was narrow, his feet were on the ground and Cinderella's eye couldn't have been more on the ball than his was.

"Roly! You idiot!"

The agonised shout came from his left back, Jenny Thorpe. And Roly knew why.

In trying to remember all the complicated rules of goalkeeping he'd forgotten – yet again – the simplest of the lot: keep your legs together.

The ball had skidded through his hands, through his open legs and straight into the net!

"If you do that tomorrow morning we'll be sunk," said Jenny.

"Redville Rockets will be out of the Inter-Schools Cup in the first round," added Ian 'Max' Maxwell, Redville's right back.

Still in their football kit, the three of them were walking home after training.

"I know," said Roly. He kicked unhappily at a stone. "I just can't stop doing it."

11

"Why don't you try hypnotising yourself?" suggested Max. "Keep saying, 'I will keep my legs together, I will keep my legs together...' "

"And fall asleep in the middle of the game?" said Jenny. "Great idea!"

"It's all right for you two," sighed Roly, "but us goalkeepers have a lot to think about. We've got to narrow our angles, stay on our feet..."

"Making sure they're next to each

other," said Jenny. "Maybe you should tie your bootlaces together, Roly."

"Hey, that could be it!" Max had stopped, a strange look in his eyes. "I mean, that's how my grandad trains his runner beans. I've seen him. He ties 'em against these canes and, bingo, after a while they grow that way."

Jenny smiled. Max wasn't known as 'Mad Max' for nothing. "After a while? Our game's tomorrow morning, remember."

"It could be worth a try though," said Roly, chewing his lip.

"It could?" said Max. He'd never had anybody say that about one of his ideas before.

"What have I got to lose?" said Roly. "I mean, I've got all evening..."

"All night if you keep your boots on in bed," pointed out Max.

"And by tomorrow morning – well, even if they're not fully trained, my legs should at least be thinking of staying together."

"Hang on, hang on. I've got it!" They'd reached Max's front gate. "Hang on right there!"

Off he dashed, up the path and into his house. Moments later he was back, and looking really pleased with himself.

"Forget lace-tying, Roly!" he said, handing over a pair of silvery rings joined by a solid length of chain. "Use these. Much more reliable."

"Handcuffs?" said Jenny.

"Not handcuffs. Footcuffs!" Max beamed. "Before my grandad retired, he was a policeman. He gave me these. I knew they'd come in useful one day!"

Roly looked at the handcuffs and then at Max. "You mean..."

"Sure thing. Put *them* round your ankles, Roly. I bet by tomorrow morning your legs'll be the best of friends!"

Roly went into his back garden the moment he got home.

He slipped one silver ring round his right ankle and the other round his left. He clicked them shut.

He stood up, slowly – and then fell down quickly as the strong chain stopped his feet from moving too far apart. Brilliant!

He picked himself up and tried again. This time he shuffled a few steps before

falling into a bush. He tried again and ended up in the hedge. Once he took a spectacular dive into the compost heap. But by teatime he'd started to get the hang of it.

Rolling his socks down over the footcuffs, Roly hopped indoors for his tea. Then, explaining to his amazed mum and dad that he had a big game tomorrow and needed an early night, he hopped upstairs to his room. There he spent the rest of the evening shuffling round in circles before falling, boots and all, into bed.

Roly got up bright and early next morning and had already managed a few laps round the garden when the doorbell went. It was Max.

"How's it going? Good idea?"

"Brilliant!" said Roly. "If this hasn't taught my legs to stay together, nothing will."

"Excellent," said Max, "and Dr Maxwell's treatment isn't over yet, Roly-boy. Look!"

Standing at the front gate, and looking very doubtful about it all, was Jenny. With a wheelbarrow.

"Personal transport to the ground," said Max. "You get in, Roly, and we'll push. That way you can keep those footcuffs on till the last minute."

And so it wasn't until he'd been trundled right into the Redville changing rooms that Roly hopped out and asked Max for the key to unlock the footcuffs.

"Key?" said Max. "What do you want a key for?"

"We need a key, Maxwell, to let him free!" bellowed Sidney 'Knees-Up' Knebworth, Redville's games teacher and the team's trainer. His blood pressure was rising almost as fast as his knees did whenever he ran on to the pitch to slosh cold water over an injured player. "This match is going to be hard enough, without having a kangaroo for a goalkeeper!"

"My grandad never gave me any key," wailed Max. "I never needed one."

"Then how did you get them off?" stormed Knees-Up.

"Just ... sort of ... slipped my hands out through the holes."

"Through the holes?" echoed Jenny. "Max ... how long's it been since you used these?"

"Ages," admitted Max. "Not since I was about four."

"Somebody, help!" moaned Roly. "We kick off in two minutes. What am I going to do?"

"The only thing you can do," said Knees-Up. "Play in them – and let's hope the ball doesn't come anywhere near you!"

And until late in the second half it didn't.

"Kick it off, kick it out, kick it anywhere - just don't let it near Roly!"

These had been Knees-Up's final instructions and the Redville players had followed them to the letter. With two minutes to go it was 0 - 0, and Roly hadn't touched the ball once.

Then the opposing team, Ripley Rangers, broke down the right. For the first time in the game their winger managed to get past Jenny Thorpe. Not for long, though. Chasing back hard, Jenny won the ball with a fine tackle. But

the Ripley winger was still breathing down her neck.

"Jenny!" called Roly, shuffling out from his goal.

Jenny shaped to pass the ball back. Then, remembering Knees-Up's instructions, she decided she'd better whack it off for a corner instead. The result was that she did a bit of both – and hit it like a bullet towards the Redville goal!

21

Roly moved his right foot. He moved his left. Right, left, right, left, until he was shuffling at top speed. It was no good. He wasn't going to make it.

Suddenly Knees-Up's words came back to him. "This match is going to be hard enough without having a kangaroo for a goalkeeper!"

A kangaroo!

Roly stopped shuffling and started hopping. Hop, hop, hop, he went, each hop taking him higher than the one before, until he sailed into a dive and fisted the ball away for a corner.

"Great save, Roly!" yelled Jenny.

"Well done, Roly-boy," said Max. "Best save you've made all season."

Over came the corner. Max headed the ball clear, but only as far as a Ripley player standing on the edge of the penalty area. Back came the ball, whistling low and hard through the ruck of players.

Roly hardly saw it. He started to bend down, but before he knew it the ball had gone through his hands - and smacked against his chained-together legs! Gratefully, he grabbed it with both hands.

"Another great save, Roly!" yelled Jenny.

"Roly!!!!" screamed another voice, much further away.

Roly looked up. It was Redville's striker, Winston Carter. In their excitement

23

the Ripley team had all charged upfield, leaving him on his own.

Could a kangaroo kick as well? Roly bounced the ball hard on the ground. Then, as it came down, he launched both feet up to meet it.

Wallop! Away sailed the ball, over the heads of the startled Ripley players and straight into the path of the galloping Winston, who had only to run on and belt it past the Ripley keeper.

"Goal!" screamed Roly. He leapt for joy. He turned a somersault. Then, as the final whistle went, he ran round his goal area in delight. Suddenly he stopped.

Leaping? Somersaulting? Running? Roly looked down at his ankles. The handcuffs had sprung open. He was free.

"It must have happened when you kicked the ball downfield," said Jenny, as everybody crowded round to congratulate Roly on his performance.

"Ah, now I remember!" cried Max. "That's how my grandad used to get them open. He gave them a whack!"

"Now he tells me," said Roly.

"All right, all right," said Max with a grin. "But admit it, Roly, you really got it together in that game."

"True," said Roly. "And we're in Round 2!"

REDVILLE ROCKETS V. BURRFIELD BLUES
The Lucky Sock

"Shorts. Shirt. Left boot. Right boot ..."

"Katherine! Have you packed your bag yet? Jason's here."

Katie Sparks sighed. "Just doing it, Mum," she called.

She blew her runny nose then, turning her sports bag upside-down, she emptied her kit onto the floor.

"Try again," muttered Katie. "Shorts. Shirt. Left boot. Right boot. Right shin-pad. Left shin-pad ... ohhh, Jason!"

Her door had opened and Jason Legge had marched in, trampling on her bag in the process.

"What's your problem?" he said as Katie started beating her fists on the floor.

"Now I've got to start packing my bag all over again."

28

"Er ... why?" said Jason.

"Because," said Katie, tipping her kit out, "if it's not packed in the right order it brings me bad luck."

"What a lot of superstitious nonsense," said Mrs Sparks, poking her head round the door.

"No it's not," said Katie, giving her nose another blow. "Before the first round I packed my socks first and my shin-pads last. And what happened?"

"We won,'" said Jason.

"But I had bad luck, didn't I? Don't you remember my shot – the one that was going straight for goal when it hit the referee on the head?"

"Sounds more like bad luck for the referee than for you" said Mrs Sparks. "Now do get a move on."

29

Katie began to pack her bag for the third time.

"Shorts. Shirt. Left boot. Right boot. Right shin-pad. Left shin-pad. Right sock. Left ..." She looked around anxiously. "Mum — have you seen my left sock?"

"Which one?"

"Which one? The dirty one with the big hole in the side, of course!"

"No, I haven't seen it," said Mrs Sparks. "And by the sounds of it I'd have thrown it away if I had."

"But it's my lucky sock! I made that hole scoring a brilliant goal. That's why I always pack it last and unpack it first. And now I can't find it!" She began a frantic search under her bed.

"Maybe you left it at school," said Jason.

Katie looked up, horror-stricken. "You're right! I did! I remember now. I ran through a puddle during practice and got it soaked. I put it on the changing room radiator to dry."

"Then it'll still be there," said Jason.

Katie snatched up her sports bag. "It had better be," she said. "Without that sock, I'll have bad luck all day."

"You don't really think that?"

"Oh no?" said Katie, pulling out her handkerchief again. "Look, it's started already. My cold's getting worse."

31

"It's not here! It's not here!" Katie was staring helplessly at the changing room radiator. "My lucky sock. It's gone!"

"Okay, don't panic. It must be around somewhere."

But it wasn't. After ten minutes' frantic searching, Katie slumped down on a bench. "Gone," she groaned. She gave her nose another blow. "I might as well not get changed at all."

"Hang on," said Jason. Making sure that Katie didn't see, he fished something out of his own sports bag and shoved it up his jumper. "I'll ... er ... have a look outside."

In the corridor he bumped into the Redville substitute, Edwin Leek, carrying the team's first-aid kit under his arm.

"Edwin," said Jason, pulling out the spare football sock he'd taken from his bag, "have you got a pair of scissors in there?"

He had. As Edwin looked on open-mouthed, Jason swiftly snipped a large hole in the side of his sock. Then he bent down and dusted the floor with it.

"Perfect," he said.

"Very shiny," said Edwin, looking at the floor.

"Not the floor, Edwin," said Jason, holding up the now filthy sock, "this."

33

Back he went to the changing room, where Katie was still looking disconsolately at the ground. "Hey, look!" he said, thrusting his hand through the sock's hole. "I've found it!"

Katie's face lit up. "Jason! You're a genius! Where was it?"

"Er ... never mind about that. Just put it on, quick! Burrfield are already on their way out to the pitch!"

Quickly, Katie put the sock on. She pulled it up. She turned over the top. And stopped.

"This isn't my lucky sock," she said. "My cold's getting worse and I'm not going to have a good game and this isn't my lucky sock."

"What do you mean?" yelled Jason. "Who else has got a disgusting sock like that? Of course it's your lucky sock!"

"Oh, yes?" Katie bent down and turned over the top. "So how come it's got your name tag sewn into it?"

As the game got under way, Katie seemed to be right. In between nose-blows, nothing was going right.

She missed the ball instead of trapping it. She had shots which hit the corner flag. Then, worst of all, she made a bad pass and gave the ball away to the Burrfield right back. As the right back stormed down the wing, Jenny Thorpe found herself outnumbered two to one. Ramon Gupta moved across to help, but that only left a gap in the middle – a gap into which the Burrfield striker ran to meet his right back's cross and head it neatly past Roly Bentall into the net.

After that, the only thing about Katie which ran well was her nose.

As the half-time whistle blew, Jason scurried over to join her. "You're right," he said angrily, "without that sock you're no good at all. You're rubbish!"

Katie looked at him. "Rubbish?" Her eyes lit up. "Rubbish! Why didn't I think of that before! Thanks, Jason!"

As the astonished Redville players watched, Katie dashed off the pitch and back towards the school buildings.

Friday night was serious cleaning night at the school, she'd just remembered. So if her lucky sock had slipped off the radiator and on to the floor, say, and been found by a cleaner and mistaken for a bit of old rubbish, say, then it would have ended up ....

This rubbish bin! thought Katie as she skidded to a halt beside a giant round metal bin on wheels.

Grabbing hold of the rim, she clambered up the side and looked over the top. Yes! It was there! She could just see it, peeking out from beneath a layer of potato peelings and what looked like school dinner leftovers.

The trouble was, she couldn't reach it. Over on the playing field, the referee's whistle blew, calling the teams together for the second half. She had to act fast. Without another thought, Katie heaved herself up and leapt into the bin.

She got back on the pitch just as the teams were lining up again.

Her nose was still blocked up, but that didn't matter. Nothing did – because on her left leg, old and tatty and covered in stains, was her lucky sock!

"Gimme the ball!" she screamed as Redville kicked off. So Jason didn't believe in the power of her lucky sock, eh? She'd show him.

As the ball arrived at her feet, Katie surged forward. The Burrfield left- back came towards her. For a moment Katie thought he was going to get to the ball first, but no. As she got near him, the defender simply stopped dead. Katie ran on. Another Burrfield defender came across to meet her. He hesitated too. They all did.

Katie looked up and saw Jason darting into the penalty area. Still nobody tried to tackle her. Completely unchallenged, all she had to do was chip the ball over for Jason to head into the net!

1–1!

"There you are!" she yelled as Jason ran over. "Now tell me this sock isn't lucky!"

Jason didn't argue. "Er ... better get on with the game," was all he said before haring away to his position on the other wing.

Sulking, thought Katie as the teams lined up again. He knows I'm right. And she hadn't finished yet.

As a Burrfield attack broke down, Roly Bentall gathered the ball and threw it out to Katie.

She set off on a run, weaving her way through the Burrfield defence. They're scared stiff of me, she thought as, one after the other, their players appeared almost to be getting out of her way. On and on she went until, suddenly, she had only the Burrfield keeper to beat.

He came out. She ran forward. He stopped. Katie went one way ... and he dived the other! Katie had only to tap the ball into the empty net.

Burrfield 1, Lucky Sock 2!

As the final whistle went, Katie ran over to Jason.

"6–1!" she yelled. "And I scored four! Now tell me my lucky sock didn't make a difference!"

"Your lucky sock didn't make a difference," said Jason, backing away.

"What!"

"It was where you found it that made the difference," said Tonsils Thomas, holding his nose. Around him, the rest of the Redville team were doing the same.

Katie lifted her football shirt to her bunged-up nose and sniffed. Faintly, she caught the most awful rubbish bin smell –

a smell that the others had obviously been getting full blast.

"You mean ..."

"It wasn't that the Burrfield defenders couldn't get near you," said Jason, "it was because they didn't want to!"

Katie sat on the ground and removed her lucky sock. She held it at arm's length all the way back to the school rubbish bin.

"Goodbye, lucky sock," said Jason as she dropped it in.

A bright smile spread across Katie's face. "But hello, Round 3!"

REDVILLE ROCKETS V. COMPTON COLTS

Cannonball Carter in Love

43

"Anyone want my dinner? I don't feel very hungry."

A hush fell over the dining hall. Winston 'Cannonball' Carter not hungry? This was unheard of.

"You feeling all right, Cannonball?" said Matt Pickup. Redville's right midfielder placed his hand on Winston's forehead.

"We don't want you going down with the lurgie, Cannonball," said Edwin Leek, the team's permanent substitute, "not with the third-round game against Compton coming up."

Everybody at the table nodded. Compton were Redville's deadly local rivals. If they lost to them, they'd never hear the last of it.

"I'm okay," said Winston. "I just don't feel so hungry nowadays, that's all." And with that he drifted dreamily out of the dining hall.

Matt Pickup shook his head solemnly. "This is serious. Cannonball going without food is like a car going without petrol. He's gonna conk out, you watch."

Matt was right. The Friday after-school training session was a disaster. Time and time again, Cannonball was put through only to hit his shot wide or to hit it so weakly that it dribbled along the ground.

"Told you," said Matt in the changing room afterwards. "Our cat could have kicked the ball harder than Cannonball."

"I can't understand it," said Edwin.

"Usually the net's in danger when Cannonball gets going. Whatever is the matter with him?"

"I know." It was Ben Wilkins, Redville's left midfielder and a walking scruff-bag. "He's in love."

"He's in what?" cried Edwin.

"Love," said Ben. "With a girl called Miranda. I've seen him when she walks past the end of our road. He goes all gooey-eyed."

"Well, if he's all gooey-eyed tomorrow we've had it," said Edwin.

Matt said, "We can't get knocked out of the cup by Compton. Anybody but them." He began to pace up and down. Suddenly he stopped. "Hey! How about if this Miranda turned up tomorrow – that would inspire Cannonball, wouldn't it?"

"What, go round her house and invite her to the game?" said Edwin. "Good thinking! Where does she live, Ben?"

Ben Wilkins shrugged. "Dunno. She doesn't go to this school, I know that."

"What does she look like?" asked Matt. "That's the important thing."

"Long hair," said Ben, thinking hard, "brownie colour. Wears a coat with a furry collar. And boots. Long boots."

"Who cares?" said Edwin. "If we don't know where she lives, we can't invite her ..."

Matt interrupted him. "We don't actually *need* her to be at the game, do we? What we need is for Cannonball to see somebody who *looks* like her. So, if we can get hold of a coat with a furry collar and a pair of boots ..."

"And a wig," said Ben, getting the idea.

"The Drama Room!" cried Edwin. "We'd find all that stuff in with the stage props!"

"...then," continued Matt, "if Cannonball's having a bad game tomorrow, somebody can get changed into it all and pretend to be this Miranda come to watch him!"

"But who?" asked Edwin. "I mean, it couldn't be you or Ben. You'll be playing in the match. It'd have to be somebody who wasn't play..."

The penny had dropped.

"Not ... me?"

"Substitute, Edwin. You're not going to be playing, so you *could* be watching!"

"Oh, no," said Edwin. "No. Not me. Definitely, definitely not ..."

"I feel stupid," said Edwin, adjusting the wig and looking in the mirror.

"You *look* stupid, Edwin," said Ben, leaning out from the door of the boys' toilets to make sure nobody was coming.

"But it's all in a good cause," said Matt. He looked at his watch. Not long to kick-

49

off. "Now, you're sure you've got Plan Miranda straight?"

"Yes," groaned Edwin, pulling off the wig, coat and boots. "I take this lot out with me in a carrier bag and hide it behind one of the trees near the gates. Then, if Cannonball's not playing well, I have to sneak away from Knees-Up and put it all on."

"Then wander about a bit till Cannonball spots you," prompted Matt.

"And bangs in some inspired goals," said Ben. "Then it's back to your place on the touchline. Right?"

Edwin Leek sighed. "Right. But I don't have to do it if Cannonball's not playing as badly as he did in the practice yesterday. Agreed?"

"Agreed."

As the first half wore on, it became clearer and clearer to Edwin that Winston 'Cannonball' Carter wasn't playing as badly as he'd played the day before.

He was playing much, much worse.

He sliced one shot towards the corner flag. He screwed another shot towards the other corner flag. Finally, when he did hit a shot cleanly, it went so high that the laughing Compton goalkeeper pretended to be watching it through a pair of binoculars as it sailed over his crossbar.

As the ball was being retrieved, Matt dashed over to the touchline, pretending to have something in his eye. "Plan Miranda," he hissed to Edwin. "Now!"

Making sure that Knees-Up Knebworth didn't see him, Edwin stole down to where his carrier bag was hidden. With a heavy heart he slipped on the coat and boots, then pulled the long-haired wig on to his head. Finally he slid out through a gap in the fence, along the short stretch of pavement...and in again through the playing field gate.

As he did so, Matt Pickup ran over to Winston and nudged him. Ben joined in, pointing in Edwin's direction. The effect on Winston was dramatic.

His chest swelled. His head lifted. His eyes glinted. His chin took on a new and determined look.

Moments later - like a hurricane in a hurry - Cannonball Carter was off and running, the ball at his toes.

A Compton defender came in to tackle him. Crunch! He bounced away as though he'd been hit by a tank.

Two more Compton defenders charged in. Winston swerved – and the defenders clattered into each other!

The Compton goalie rushed out, but Winston gave him no chance at all. The ball hammered past him and into the net as if it had been fired from a gun.

1–0 to Redville!

Standing on the touchline, the lovely Edwin forgot himself. He leapt in the air. He skipped with delight. He turned a cartwheel. Finally, and it would have to be just as Winston looked his way, he yanked

his wig off and threw it into the air.

As Winston realised that he'd been fooled, his chest capsized, his eyes lost their glint and, as for his chin, it might as well have been on the floor.

He started playing worse than ever. Trudging back to help out his defence, Winston lost the ball in his own penalty area. A quick shot and Compton were level at 1–1.

A couple of minutes later Compton were ahead as Winston, trying to pass back to Ramona Gupta, hit the ball straight to the feet of the Compton striker, who only had to tap it past Roly Bentall and into the Redville goal.

2-1 to Compton.

"There can't be long to go," puffed Matt Pickup as Compton began to run the game. "I reckon we're out."

Ben Wilkins nodded. "We need a miracle," he gasped.

"Like ..." began Matt. He stopped, open-mouthed, looking towards the gate. "That!" he gasped.

Ben turned to look. A girl with long hair and a coat with a furry collar had just come through the gate and was standing, watching the match.

"Cannonball!" he yelled. "Look! It's Miranda! It's really her!"

"Oh, yeah?" said Winston.

Ben pointed again, this time at Edwin Leek, standing on the touchline. "See? Edwin's there. It must be her!"

Winston looked towards the gate. He looked at Edwin. He looked towards the gate again. It was *her*! It was!

The Redville striker played the last ten minutes of the match like a boy on fire.

He picked up the ball in the centre-circle. Brushing off tackle after tackle, he ploughed on into the Compton penalty area. He pretended he was going to hit the hardest shot of his life and then, as the Compton goalie dived out of the way in fear, he simply tapped the ball into the net with a laugh!

No sooner had Compton kicked off than Winston got the ball again. This time, as the Compton defenders backed off, he *did* hit the hardest shot of his life. From fully thirty metres out, he let fly. Whoosh! The shot went like a rocket, straight at the Compton goalie. Thwack! He caught it - only to be sent staggering backwards and over his own goal-line!

3–2 to Redville!

"Well, that must have impressed her," said Matt Pickup as the final whistle went and

Winston trotted over to where Miranda was still standing.

Over by the gate, though, the conversation didn't last long. In next to no time, Winston was walking back.

"What did Miranda say, Cannonball?" called Matt.

"Enjoy the match, did she?" said Ben.

"Nope," said Winston seriously.

"No?" said Matt. "No? She sees you bang in a hat-trick and she's not impressed? What did she want, blood?"

"Nope," said Winston. "She wanted Compton to win. That's the school she goes to!"

"Then ... why did she come to watch you?" said Ben.

"And why didn't she say she was going to?" said Edwin Leek, giving his carrier bag of disguise an angry kick.

"She *didn't* come to watch me," said Winston. He pointed over to where Miranda was helping to his feet a boy clutching his stomach. "She came to watch their goalie!"

"Ooops!" said Matt.

59

"I'm sorry, Cannonball," said Ben.

"Well, I'm not," said Winston, his face breaking into a broad grin. "We're in Round 4!"

REDVILLE ROCKETS V. ST BUDE'S JUNIORS

Silence is Goalden

"It was your fault!" yelled Ramona Gupta.

"It wasn't!" her brother, Ramon, yelled back.

"It was!"

"It was not! It was your fault!"

"My fault? It wasn't my fault!"

"Was!"

"Was not!"

"And I say it was!"

"And I say it wasn't ..."

"Sounds like the twins are having a little family disagreement," said Roly Bentall.

Jenny Thorpe shrugged. "That's just their way. Some kids like playing together. Bruv and Sis like arguing."

"I wonder what they're arguing about?" said Roly, looking across the

playground to where Ramona and Ramon Gupta's noses were touching as they glared at each other.

"What do brothers and sisters usually argue about?" said Jenny.

"Dunno," shrugged Roly, who didn't have any brothers or sisters.

"Exactly. They probably don't know either."

"Well, I just hope they sort it out by Saturday," said Roly. "I don't fancy being in goal behind two central defenders who are moaning at each other all the time."

"Don't worry, Roly," said Jenny. "It's only Wednesday. It'll all be over by Saturday. Bruv and Sis's arguments never last ..."

"If you don't admit it was your fault ..." bawled Ramon Gupta.

"Oh, yes ..." hollered Ramona Gupta.

"Then I'll ..."

"What? You'll what?"

"I ... I won't talk to you again!"

"Ever?"

"No," said Ramon, thinking he was winning at last, "never!"

"Great!" cried Ramona. "And I won't talk to *you* again!"

"Right, then I won't talk to you either!"

"Right!"

"Right!"

"Well," said Roly, as he watched Bruv and Sis march out of the school gates at the end of the day, "they don't seem to be arguing any more."

"I don't think they're talking any more, Roly," said Jenny, pointing.

Ramona Gupta, head in the air, looked as if she was counting clouds. Beside her, head down, Ramon Gupta seemed to be counting paving stones.

"It doesn't look good," said Roly.

Jenny tried to sound hopeful. "It's only Thursday. They'll be nattering away to each other by tomorrow ..."

"Jenny, will you ask my brother to pass the salt please?" Jenny looked at Ramona.

"You could ask him yourself, Sis," she

said. "I mean, he is sitting next to you."

Ramon Gupta grabbed the salt cellar. He handed it to Roly, sitting opposite.

"Do us a favour, Roly. Give this to my sister. And while you're at it, ask her to pass the tomato sauce before she guzzles the lot."

"Tell my brother," snapped back Ramona, "that when it comes to tomato sauce, he's good enough to guzzle for England!"

"And you can tell my sister," Ramon yelled, "she's talking out of the top of her head!"

"And you can tell my brother ..."

"And you can tell my sister ..."

Roly and Jenny staggered out of the hall. It had been the longest lunch break they'd ever known.

"So their arguments never last, eh?" said Roly.

"They don't," said Jenny. "Not usually."

"Well, this one must be setting a record."

Jenny brightened. "Well, there you are then. Records are only broken by little bits at a time, aren't they? Look at the Olympics. No, they'll be over it by tomorrow."

"I hope you're right," said Roly. "Tomorrow is Saturday, remember. The fourth round of the cup against St Bude's..."

But, as the game got under way the next morning, Jenny soon discovered that, far from getting better, things were actually getting worse.

After a long spell of Redville pressure, St Bude's broke away. Latching on to a long ball down the middle, their striker ran towards Ramon and Ramona.

"Tell my brother to go and tackle him!" Ramona shouted to Jenny.

"Tell my sister to tackle him herself!" shouted Ramon. "I'll cover."

"Tell my brother," yelled Ramona, stopping dead and putting her hands on

her hips, "that he's nearer. So he can tackle and I'll cover!"

Ramon stopped dead too. "Tell my sister ..."

It was too late to tell anybody anything. As the twins stopped still, the St Bude's striker darted between them and ran into the Redville penalty area.

Jenny Thorpe dashed across to tackle him. Roly Bentall charged out of his goal.

But they were both too late. The St Bude's striker shot – and watched in despair as his shot clipped the post and went off for a goal kick!

"0–0," said Roly as they trudged off at half-time. "Our luck can't last."

"Not unless Bruv and Sis start talking again," gasped Jenny, breathless through running around and passing messages.

"I can't see that happening," said Roly. "Look at them."

Ramon and Ramona Gupta hadn't come over to the touchline for their half-time oranges. They were still standing on the edge of the penalty area. Ramon, his arms folded, was looking one way. Ramona, her arms folded, had her back to him and was facing the other way.

"I mean," said Roly, "who'd believe they're supposed to be on the same side?"

"On the same side," said Jenny thoughtfully. "Roly, I've just had an idea!"

As Ramon and Ramona stood on the pitch ignoring each other, Jenny told Roly what she'd thought of.

"Hey! It could work!" said Roly.

Quickly they gathered the rest of the team together.

"Okay?" said Jenny, after explaining her plan. "As soon as one of us gets the chance, that's what we'll do ...'

The chance Jenny had talked about came along ten minutes into the second half. As a St Bude's attack broke down, Ramon Gupta got the ball.

"Bruv!" called Jenny.

71

Ramon slid a pass straight to her. As the ball came, Jenny deliberately ran too far forward.

"That was a useless pass!" she yelled as the ball rolled off for a throw-in. "Totally useless!"

"What do you mean?" said Ramon. "It was straight to you."

The plan swung into action.

"No, it wasn't, Bruv," shouted Roly from his goal, "it was a hopeless pass!"

"Rubbish!" yelled Max Maxwell from right back.

"A load of toffee!" called Matt Pickup from midfield.

Everybody else joined in.

"Pathetic, Bruv!"

"Pitiful!"

"My granny could do better!"

Everybody else, that is, except Ramona Gupta.

With a yell of, 'Stop picking on my brother!' she dashed across as St Bude's took their throw-in. Winning a good tackle, she pushed the ball forward to Ben Wilkins, who then tripped over it on purpose.

"Useless, Sis!" shouted Ben. "How am I supposed to do anything with a pass like that!"

Once again, everybody else joined in.

"You'd get a straighter pass from a banana!"

"Or a corkscrew!"

And again, only one voice disagreed. "Stop picking on my sister!" yelled Ramon. Dashing forward, he won the ball and passed it – to Ramona.

"Come on, Sis! Let's show 'em!"

"Right, Bruv!" shouted Ramona.

She moved forward to collect Ramon's pass, waited until a St Bude's player came in to tackle her and then passed it back to Ramon again.

On they went.

Ramon to Ramona.

Ramona to Ramon.

On down the field, swapping passes, until they reached the St Bude's penalty area. Out came the goalkeeper.

Ramon to Ramona, Ramona to Ramon – and they were past him with the ball between them!

"Go on, Sis," called Ramon.

"Go on, Bruv," called Ramona.

Ramona swung her left foot. Ramon swung his right foot. And together they hit the ball into the empty net!

"That was close," said Jenny as the game ended with Redville 1 – 0 winners.

"At least we won," said Roly. "Thanks to you and your plan."

Behind him, Ramon and Ramona Gupta were walking off the pitch with their arms round each other.

"Well played, Sis," said Roly.

"And you, Bruv," said Jenny.

"Thanks," said Ramon. "Did you like the goal I scored?"

Ramona gave her brother a look. "The goal *you* scored? You mean the goal *I* scored?"

"You? I scored that goal."

"You did not!"

"I did!"

"Ohhhh!" yelled Jenny. "Stop arguing! We're in Round 5!"

REDVILLE ROCKETS V. PRIDWELL PRIDE

Right Back - Behind the Goal

Ben Wilkins dribbled his moth-eaten tennis ball through the school gates, across the playground, through a set of swing doors, along a corridor, up to his classroom door - and bumped into Mr Knebworth.

The teacher looked down. He took off his spectacles, gave them a quick polish on his tie, put them back on and looked down again. The sight hadn't improved. "Benjamin Wilkins," he said, "go and tidy yourself up."

Ben strolled off to the boys' toilets. There, he inspected himself in the mirror. He saw his hair, looking as if he'd borrowed it from a hedgehog; his Redville top, all ragged and tatty through forever being used as a goal post; his trousers,

with big muddy splodges showing where he'd knelt down to fish his tennis ball out of a hedge; and his shoes, a nice mud colour all over. He frowned.

"Tidy myself up?" he said to himself. "What's ol' Knees-Up on about?"

And so, doing no more than stick a small section of his hair down with a dab of water, Ben headed back to class.

Mr Knebworth was not in a particularly good mood.

His old watch had stopped again, making him late. Then his car had refused to start and he'd made himself filthy getting it going. By the time he'd arrived in school and tidied himself up, he'd been too late to get the refreshing cup of tea he needed to begin the day.

And now, as he sat in Registration, dying of thirst because he'd taken the trouble to make himself look respectable, what did he see arriving? Ben Wilkins, looking like a scarecrow after a stormy night in a muddy field.

"Detention, Benjamin Wilkins!" bellowed Mr Knebworth. "I told you to tidy yourself up!"

Ben looked at him. His face fell. "What?"

"Detention," repeated Mr Knebworth. "Tomorrow night. After school"

"Tomorrow?" echoed Ben. "After school?"

"Correct."

There was a stunned silence. Then uproar.

"You can't!" shouted Jason Legge. "Not tomorrow!"

Mr Knebworth swung round in his chair. "I can, Jason. And you can join him! Detention for you tomorrow as well!"

"What!" yelled Max Maxwell. "You don't know what you're doing!"

This was too much for Mr Knebworth. "I don't know what I'm doing?" he roared. "*I* don't know what I'm doing?" He leapt to his feet. "Well, let me tell you, Ian Maxwell, that I know *exactly* what I'm doing. You're in detention too! All three of you. Straight after school tomorrow. Three-fifteen, on the dot!"

And with that he stomped off towards the staffroom to collect the books he needed for the first lesson.

He met Steve 'Tonsils' Thomas on the way.

"All go for tomorrow, Mr Knebworth," Redville's captain said brightly. "No injuries reported."

Mr Knebworth strode past, then stopped. "Tomorrow?" he said, turning round slowly.

"The Cup match," said Tonsils. "Against Pridwell. Remember? They couldn't play this Saturday, so you rearranged it for after school tomorrow."

"Remember?" Mr Knebworth gave a little laugh. "Ha-ha. Of course I do. Er ... remind me, Stephen, what time did I say the kick-off was?"

"Three-thirty."

"Now what do we do?" said Jason. "The game'll be half over by the time we get there. We'll be 10 – 0 down."

"I think we should go and plead with Knees-Up," said Max.

"Right," said Ben. "Knees down – on the ground."

So at break they pleaded. But it did no good. As the three of them stood in front of him, Mr Knebworth shook his head.

"My decision is final," he said. "I couldn't possibly let you off. Not after giving you detentions in front of the whole class." He gave a deep sigh. "It is going to hurt me as much as it hurts you three, you know."

"Oh, yes?" said Jason. "How?"

"I am going to have to supervise you,"

said the teacher. "The game will have to start without me too."

"Tactics!" said Jason.

"Tactics?" said Max. "What are you on about? We're going to miss the match."

"You don't need tactics in detention," added Ben.

"But you do need them for getting *out* of detention," said Jason. "So come on, think! How can we do it?"

"We can't. You heard old Knees-Up. He isn't going to change his mind. We're not going to get out of it. We're going to be late for the match."

Jason snapped his fingers. "Hey! That's it! We don't need to get *out* of detention . We just need to get out of it *early*!"

"Early?" said Ben.

85

"Early!" repeated Jason. "Detention starts at three-fifteen, right?"

"And finishes at four o'clock ..."

"Forget that. The match starts at three-thirty. So, if we can get out of detention after fifteen minutes we'll be in time for the kick off!"

"After fifteen minutes?" said Ben. "Thirty minutes early? And how d'you think we're going to talk Knees-Up into that?"

Jason's face broke into a huge grin. "We're not," he said. "His old watch is always going wrong, isn't it? All we have to do is persuade him it's gone wrong again."

"And how are we going to do that, Mastermind?" asked Max.

"Easy," said Jason. "We're going to change the detention room clock!"

As the desk he was balancing on wobbled dangerously, Jason flattened himself against the detention room wall and with a lunge managed to flick the clock down from the screw it was hanging on.

Ben caught it safely. Turning it over, he saw the little knob that adjusted the hands. Quickly he moved them on so that the clock said three–forty instead of three–ten. He gave it back to Jason. A wobbly tiptoe and a stretch later, it was back on the wall.

"We need to cover it up with something," said Max. "If Knees-Up sees a clock telling him there's only fifteen minutes to go before we've started he'll smell a rat, won't he?"

"Good point," said Jason. "Take your football shirt off, Ben. We'll cover it with that."

"What?" said Ben. They'd nearly broken their necks dashing out of class to get changed as soon as the bell went, and here he was being told to get unchanged again. "Why me?"

"Because you got us into this mess, that's why," said Max. "Anyway, you've got the biggest football shirt."

Ben pulled his shirt off and handed it up. Jason stretched once more, threw Ben's shirt over the clock's plastic face and leapt down. By the time Mr Knebworth arrived, on the dot of three-fifteen, the three of them were sitting at their desks, trying to look innocent.

"Benjamin," said Mr Knebworth immediately, "is your football shirt hanging from the clock for a reason?"

"Er ... " stammered Ben.

He thought quickly. "It's drying, Sir. Me mum washed it last night – this being a big match and all."

"Ah. Quite," said Mr Knebworth. He sighed. "An unfortunate situation all round. Still, let's make the best of it. You three can do some homework, while I do some marking." And with that he buried his head in the big pile of books he'd brought with him.

Jason started counting seconds under his breath. "Elephant one, elephant two, elephant three ..." until he reached "elephant sixty". He raised a finger as Ben and Jason looked his way. One minute gone.

"Elephant one, elephant two ..."

Five minutes went by. Then eight. Ten. Twelve. Thirteen. Fourteen. Fifteen. As Jason stuck his thumb up dramatically, Ben leaned back and tugged at his shirt.

"Mr Knebworth, can we go now?" he heard Jason say.

Max joined in. "Time's up, Mr Knebworth."

Up at the front, Mr Knebworth still had his head down. Any moment now he would be looking up at the clock. And what would he see? Nothing, realised Ben. His tug hadn't moved the shirt at all. It was stuck!

He gave it another tug. Then another.

"Look at the clock, Mr Knebworth," he heard Jason say. "The time is ..."

Ben panicked. He gave his shirt one last, almighty tug – and pulled it free! He looked triumphantly at Jason. And heard him say, "I don't know what the time is."

In his panic, Ben had not only pulled his shirt down but the clock's perspex cover and its minute hand! It was impossible to tell the time from it.

"Hmm," said Mr Knebworth, finally looking up. "Well, I make it ..." He pulled out his ancient watch – " four o'clock. Off you go. And good luck!"

How could his time-counting have been so bad? thought Jason as they charged out on to the pitch. The teams were lining up to kick off. They must have missed the whole of the first half!

"What's the score?" he asked as he dashed to his position alongside Tonsils Thomas.

"What do you think it is?" said Tonsils. "0 – 0. We haven't started yet."

On the touchline, Knees-Up Knebworth watched as Max Maxwell sent Ben Wilkins off on yet another mazy dribble. Past one Pridwell player, then past another, a quick one-two with Jason Legge, into the penalty area and - wallop! Into the net for Redville's fourth goal and his hat trick.

"Ben's playing brilliantly, isn't he, Mr Knebworth?" said Edwin Leek at his side. "Think he's got time to score another one, do you?"

"I doubt it, Edwin," said Mr Knebworth. "There can't be more than a minute left." He pulled out his watch ... and frowned.

The game should have finished half an hour ago.

Then he remembered. Making sure that Edwin Leek couldn't see what he was doing, Knees-Up Knebworth turned his watch back by thirty minutes.

On the pitch the final whistle went.

"Well played, Redville!" shouted Mr Knebworth happily. "Next stop, the semi-finals!"

REDVILLE ROCKETS V. LANSDOWNE LIONS

It's Tough Having Your 'Tonsils' Out

"Shoot, Cannonball!"

"Get stuck in, Katie!"

"Go for it, Max!"

"Run, Jason!"

"Your ball, Sis!"

"Support her, Bruv!"

"Come out, Roly!"

"Overlap, Jenny!"

"Tackle, Pick!"

"Take him on, Ben!"

"It's a wonder," said Knees-Up Knebworth as the practice session finished, "that Stephen Thomas has got any voice left at all."

"That's why we call him 'Tonsils', Mr Knebworth," said Ramona Gupta.

"Because we see more of them than

anything else!" said her brother, Ramon.

"Well, he's certainly an inspiration," said Mr Knebworth, "and that's what I want from a captain. Mind you," he added, waggling a finger in his ear, "it would be an awful lot more peaceful without him."

Had he seen him leave the changing room a little later, Knees-Up Knebworth might have thought that Redville's captain had changed his style.

Quietly, Tonsils finished packing his bag. Quietly, he slipped away from the others. Outside, he looked round to make sure he wasn't being followed. Then, quietly, he scuttled along the corridor until he reached a door marked "Music Room". He opened the door quietly and went in.

"All ready?" he whispered.

Sitting at one of the school's keyboards, Edwin Leek nodded.

Ramon Gupta, looking up from his task of plugging a lead into the back of the ghetto-blaster he carried everywhere, grinned.

Beside him, Ramona Gupta clicked a tape into its front. She switched it on, saw its little red light glow and put her thumb up.

Edwin handed a microphone to Tonsils. "Ready to record, Captain," he said, brightly. "All you've got to do is sing!"

"Result," said Tonsils, "one team song for Monday's assembly! Are the others going to be knocked out when they hear this!"

"Assuming we win the semi-final tomorrow," said Ramona.

"I won't let us lose," said Tonsils, pulling a sheet of paper out of his sports bag. "I want this song heard on Monday. So, let's go, Edwin baby!"

As Edwin played the tune of 'Rule Britannia', Tonsils sang:

"Come on, Redville!
Oh Redville, we love you!
Others never, never, never
Will beat you!"

"What do you reckon, Tonsils?" said Ramon, after playing the tape back.

"Magic!" said Tonsils, with a cough.

Beside him, Ramona began to take the tape out of the player.

"Hey! What you doing, Sis?"

"I thought we'd finished," said Ramona.

"No, sirree!" coughed Tonsils, digging in his sports bag and lifting out a pile of paper. "I've got another eleven verses to do yet!"

"Is that it?" said Ramona, much later.

"Just one more verse," croaked Tonsils.

"You sure you can manage it?" said Ramon. "You sound like a frog with a cold."

"No problem," whispered Tonsils

hoarsely. "This one's only a joke, though. Just for the team to hear. Whatever you do, Bruv, don't play this one in Assembly!"

"Right then, Redville," snapped Mr Knebworth in the changing room the next morning. "I want to hear plenty of calling for the ball and plenty of encouragement." He pointed at Tonsils. "Follow your captain's example."

Tonsils smiled and stuck his thumb in the air.

"Anything to say to the team before we go out?" Knees-Up asked him.

Tonsils shook his head. Knees-Up gave him a look.

"You're quiet this morning, Stephen. What's the problem - lost your voice?" He chortled.

Tonsils swallowed hard, then nodded again. His lips spoke the words "Yes, Sir", but nothing came out.

"Oh," said Knees-Up. "I see. Well ... it's going to be a quiet game then, isn't it?"

And it was. As the game progressed, Tonsils managed to give the odd croak, but that was it. By half-time, with the score still at 0–0, he couldn't even manage that.

"What's the matter with you all?" Mr Knebworth said as they gathered round him. "We should be winning this game."

"It's too quiet!" said Ramona. "We can't get going without Tonsils yelling at us!"

"Well, you're going to have to, aren't you? Stephen's lost his voice. He can't

conjure one up out of thin air, you know!"
Out of thin air? Ramona looked at Edwin,
who nodded hard. He'd just had the same
thought. So had Ramon Gupta.

"Go, Edwin! It's in the changing
room!"

The game had restarted by the time Edwin
dashed back to his spot on the touchline.
Under his arm he was carrying Ramon's
ghetto-blaster, the tape they'd recorded
the day before still in it.

"Turn it on, Edwin!" yelled Ramona
Gupta.

Edwin switched the ghetto-blaster on,
turned the volume up as far as it would go
and moments later the unmistakable voice
of Tonsils Thomas was booming out
across the pitch!

"Play up, Redville!

Oh Redville, we love you!

Others never, never, never

Will beat you!"

Edwin wound the tape back and played it again. And again.

"Edwin!" gasped Knees-Up Knebworth beside him. "It's working!"

Out on the pitch, things had started happening. The Redville players were moving a bit faster. Tackles they'd been losing before they were now winning. They were getting on top.

Jason Legge hared down the wing. He slipped the ball inside to Katie Sparks. She laid it back. Wallop! Cannonball Carter hit a rocket shot. Crack! It thumped against the bar and bounced back into play.

"Much better, Redville!" hollered Knees-Up. Then, to Edwin, "Rewind, Edwin! Play it again!"

But Edwin didn't have time to rewind the tape. After surviving Cannonball's shot, Lansdowne had broken away. Their left-winger was scampering into the penalty area with a now super-enthusiastic Max Maxwell in hot pursuit.

105

Pheep! The referee's whistle shrieked.

"Penalty," groaned Mr Knebworth. In his enthusiasm, Max had lunged for the ball and ended up fouling the Lansdowne winger.

Edwin looked at his watch. "Only five minutes to go, Mr Knebworth."

Mr Knebworth nodded. "If Roly doesn't save this we're in big trouble. Let's hope he's inspired, eh?"

Inspired? Tonsils' other verses! Edwin hit the 'Fast Forward' button on the ghetto-blaster. Then he hit 'Play'.

"Come on, Roly!
We believe in you!
You can save it, save it, save it,
Go on - do!"

As Tonsils' recording boomed across to the Redville goal, Roly Bentall crouched

down with a look of fierce determination on his face. The Lansdowne captain strode up to take the kick - and saw Roly swoop to push the ball round the post!

"Well done, Edwin!" beamed Mr Knebworth. A thought struck him. "You haven't got a verse on that tape for Katie Sparks, have you? We could do with a bit of magic from her right now."

Edwin hit the Fast Foward button again. He remembered that Katie had been the last of the Redville players

Tonsils had recorded a verse for. He found the right spot on the tape just as Katie picked the ball up in midfield.

"Come on, Katie,
We know what you can do,
You can run and leave your marker
In the stew!"

With a surge of determination, Katie shot forward. Past her marker she went, then past another defender and dashed on into the Lansdowne penalty area – only to stop dead as their centre back charged in

to tackle. As he slithered past on his backside, Katie moved forward again, drew the goalie and then gently slipped the ball to one side. All Jason Legge had to do was run it into the empty net!

"Well done, you two!" said Ramona to Edwin and Ramon as the final whistle blew to leave Redville 1–0 winners.

"And well done to you too, Stephen," Mr Knebworth said as Tonsils ran over.

"That verse about me really helped," said Roly.

"And the one about me," said Katie.

Tonsils gave a hoarse laugh. "Good job you didn't play that other verse though, Edwin. You know, the one about …"

Edwin stopped him with a horrified squeak. "I didn't turn it off!"

109

They all turned – and saw Ramon Gupta's ghetto-blaster on the grass, its little red light still glowing.

"You mean ..." croaked Tonsils.

He didn't have time to finish. The last verse he'd recorded boomed out for everybody to hear.

"Knees-Up Knebworth,

O Knees-Up, we hate you!

With your sponge and icy water,

We go blue!"

As the verse finished, Mr Knebworth slowly bent down to turn off the ghetto-blaster. "Stephen Thomas," he growled as he stood up, "I have only one thing to say to you."

"Ye-ye-yes, Mr Knebworth?" stammered Tonsils.

"Redville are in the Final!"

REDVILLE ROCKETS V. JARRETT JUNIORS
Come on, Number 12!

"The Cup Final, Edwin," said Mr Knebworth. "Who would have believed it?"

"Done well, haven't they, Mr Knebworth?" said Edwin Leek with a sigh.

"They? They? What's all this 'they' business, Edwin? You mean 'we'! We – you and I, Edwin – are part of the team too, you know!"

"You are, Mr Knebworth. You're the coach and all that. But I'm only the substitute. All I've done is stand on the side."

"And carried the bucket and sponge when necessary, Edwin. A vital task."

"But how about me actually *playing*, Mr Knebworth? I mean, I haven't actually come on once yet."

"Ah." Mr Knebworth stroked his chin.

He sucked his teeth. This was tricky. Edwin was certainly keen. He was certainly enthusiastic. But there it ended. The fact was that, where football was concerned, Edwin Leek was an extremely good bucket-and-sponge carrier.

"Will I get on today, Mr Knebworth?" asked Edwin. "It would be great to get on in the Final! Will I, Mr Knebworth?"

Knees-Up coughed. "Er ... no, Edwin. I'm sorry."

As Edwin Leek glumly followed Knees-Up out of the changing room, Tonsils Thomas nudged Ramon Gupta.

"What do you think about Edwin coming on today, Bruv?"

Ramon shrugged. "Could be. If we're winning."

Matt Pickup popped his head out from between a couple of coats hanging on their hooks. "Great idea, I say – so long as there's no chance of us losing. I mean, Edwin is substitute for a reason, isn't he?"

"Because he's useless," said Tonsils. "I know. But if we're well in the lead?"

"Then it would be a lovely idea," said Jenny Thorpe, as the others voiced their agreement too.

"Okay," said Tonsils, getting to his feet. "So this is what we'll do ..."

He outlined his plan. "Okay, Jenny? Okay, everyone?"

There were nods all round. "Right then," said Tonsils. "But first we've got to get so far ahead we can't be beaten."

And they did. Redville were inspired.

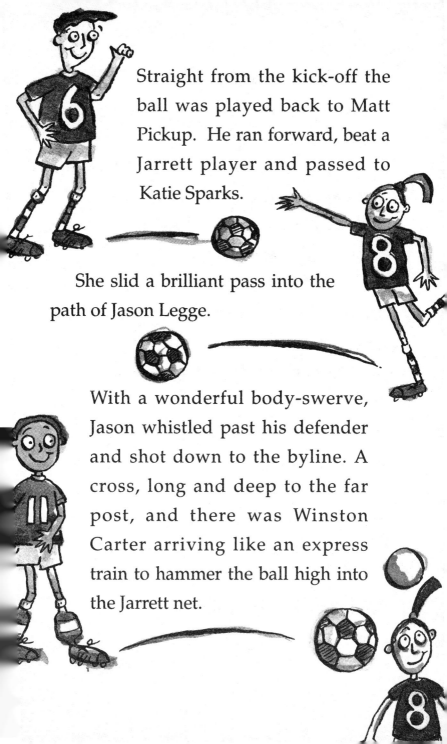

Straight from the kick-off the ball was played back to Matt Pickup. He ran forward, beat a Jarrett player and passed to Katie Sparks.

She slid a brilliant pass into the path of Jason Legge.

With a wonderful body-swerve, Jason whistled past his defender and shot down to the byline. A cross, long and deep to the far post, and there was Winston Carter arriving like an express train to hammer the ball high into the Jarrett net.

Redville 1, Jarrett 0, after only twenty seconds!

Minutes later it was 2–0. A swift interception from Ramona Gupta won the ball for Redville. She played it out to Max Maxwell, who charged down the wing before sliding the ball across to Ben Wilkins. Ben set off on a mazy dribble, the ball looking as though it was tied to his bootlace. A little pass into the Jarrett penalty box - and there was Katie Sparks, running through to bang the ball into the net!

With seconds to go before half-time, Redville hit their third. Dashing up from fullback, Jenny Thorpe won a corner. Over it came - straight on to the head of Ramon Gupta to bullet it past the Jarrett goalkeeper!

With ten minutes to go, the score was still 3–0 and Redville were coasting. Jenny Thorpe ran over to Tonsils.

"What do you think? Now?"

Tonsils thought for a second, then nodded. "Should be safe," he said. "Go for it, Jenny."

The Jarrett winger sprinted forward. He'd been having a bad time against Jenny and, once again, she slid in with a tackle and pushed the ball off for a throw-in. This time, however, she didn't get up.

"Aaggh! It's my ankle," she moaned as Knees-Up Knebworth came puffing across the pitch with Edwin behind him carrying the bucket and sponge.

"Aaaaggghhh!" she yelled even louder

as a spongeful of freezing water was sloshed on to her ankle.

"How's that?" asked Knees-Up.

"Worse," said Jenny. It was true. She'd only been pretending before - that had been the plan. Now her ankle felt like it was suffering from frostbite.

"I'll have to come off," she moaned. "Edwin will have to take my place."

Mr Knebworth's face fell. "Really?"

"Really," said Jenny. As she hopped towards the touch line, Mr Knebworth checked his watch. Ten minutes to go and 3–0 up. He looked at Edwin, then back to his watch. Finally he took a deep breath and said, "Very well. On you go, Edwin."

The match got under way again. In Jenny's position at left back, Edwin

bounced up and down. He was on the pitch at last. And in the Cup Final. Brilliant!

There was only one thing he needed now to make his day complete – a kick of the ball.

Suddenly, he saw his chance. As Ramona Gupta won the ball with another good tackle, she hit it gently back towards Roly Bentall in the Redville goal.

Thinking that he could get the kick he wanted by helping the ball on its way back to Roly, Edwin hared across the field. The trouble was that, in his hurry to get on to the field in the first place, he hadn't done his lace up very well. Now, as he thundered towards the ball, the lace slid under his foot. The effect was disastrous. Like a torpedo in football gear, Edwin dived forward, slithered along the ground - and hit the ball past Roly Bentall with his head. An own goal!

"Right ... look ... don't worry about it, Edwin," said a shaky Tonsils Thomas as the teams lined up again. "We're still 3–1 up. Forget it."

But, as he hurriedly retied his lace, Edwin couldn't forget it. It had been his big chance and he'd fluffed it. Somehow he had to make amends. But how?

Over on the far side of the field, Jarrett

had surged on to the attack again and won a corner.

"Cover the post, Edwin!" said Roly Bentall.

Edwin nodded grimly. He positioned himself. Over came the ball, swinging in towards the Redville goal. Edwin watched it coming. Roly'll catch it, he thought. Or would he? Roly Bentall didn't seem to be moving. The ball was still swinging in. Still Roly wasn't moving. He had to do something!

Dashing from his spot on the post, Edwin shot past Roly and lunged for the ball – only for it to balloon off his toe and over Roly's head for another own goal!

"You twit!" screamed Roly.

"You didn't go for it!" wailed Edwin. "Why didn't you go for it?"

"Because I could see it was going off!" yelled Roly.

"Edwin ..." It was Tonsils, now looking very shaky. "How about if I play in defence and you go into midfield, eh?"

They kicked off again. But, having pulled back to 3–2, Jarrett were on the rampage. Seizing on a loose ball, their captain surged through the middle.

Edwin braced himself. He was going to make up for everything. Jarrett's captain had to be stopped and he, Edwin Leek, was going to do it. Edwin turned and gave chase. He was getting closer! He was catching him!

The Jarrett captain pulled back his foot. He was going to shoot! With a desperate effort, Edwin stuck out his foot and booted the ball away from him - but also,

as he saw to his horror, away from Roly Bentall! The ball sailed on into the Redville goal to make the score 3–3!

Edwin had scored one of the fastest hat tricks in living memory – and all in his own goal.

"Get up front!" screamed Tonsils Thomas.

"Up front!" echoed Roly Bentall, Max Maxwell, Ramon Gupta, Ramona Gupta, Matt Pickup, Katie Sparks, Winston Carter, Jason Legge and – from the touchline, wishing she was back on the pitch – Jenny Thorpe.

"Out on the wing!" bellowed Mr Knebworth, "and out of the way!" He checked his watch. One minute to go. Could they survive extra time with Edwin

Leek in the side? Could they even *get* to extra time?

Jarrett were swarming all over Redville now. Their forwards were up. Their midfield was rampaging forward. Now, as they won a corner in the dying seconds of the game, every Jarrett defender piled forward too.

Over came the ball. This time, without Edwin in the way, Roly got to it first.

"Kick it anywhere!" yelled Tonsils.

Roly kicked it – straight down the field and into the path of Edwin, standing completely alone. Edwin hared excitedly after the ball. Could he get to it before the Jarrett goalkeeper? Could he bang into the net for the winner? That would make up for everything!

Suddenly he heard a flapping sound. His lace, done up hurriedly after his first own goal, was coming undone again. Edwin ran on.

In front of him, the Jarrett goalkeeper was coming out to meet him. As Edwin caught up with the ball, he felt his boot start to wobble. He began to stumble. What could he do? In a panic, Edwin lashed out with his foot – and made contact!

As he fell he saw the ball sail through

the air. On and on it sailed - until the Jarrett goalkeeper dived to one side and caught it!

Edwin buried his head in his hands. The final whistle had gone. All around him the Redville players were shouting and hollering.

No, they weren't! They were cheering!

"Goal! Great goal, Edwin!"

Goal? Goal? Edwin lifted his head - and saw the ball, buried in the Jarrett net. But his shot? Hadn't he seen it saved?

"Their goalie saved your boot, Edwin!"

As the Redville team crowded round, Edwin got to his feet. He felt himself being lifted on to their shoulders.

"Up you go, Edwin!" they all shouted.

"Yeh!" yelled Edwin. "Up for the Cup!"